Pokémon

BLACK & WHITE

ASH'S TRIPLE THREAT

Based on the episodes "Triple Leaders, Team Threats!" and "Dreams by the Yard Full!"

by Simcha Whitehill

ISBN 978-0-545-34169-1

12 11 10 9 8 7 6 5 4 3   11 12 13 14 15 16/0

Designed by Cheung Tai
Printed in the U.S.A.   40
First printing, September 2011

SCHOLASTIC INC.

New York	Toronto	London	Auckland
Sydney	Mexico City	New Delhi	Hong Kong

Ash, Pikachu, and their new friend Iris were on the road to Striaton City.

"I can't wait for my first Gym battle in Unova!" Ash said.

"Hope you know where the Gym is!" Iris said.

Just then, a young man with green hair walked by. "An Axew!" he said. "And whoa, it's a Pikachu! You've got a rare Pokémon, you know!"

"We're from Kanto. My name's Ash, and Pikachu's my partner!" Ash said.

"Hi, I'm Cilan, a Pokémon connoisseur!" the young man said.

"Pokémon connoisseur? What's that?" Ash replied.

"I help Trainers and their Pokémon get to know each other," Cilan said.

"Do you know where the Striaton Gym is?" Ash asked Cilan. "I'm here to challenge it!"

"Let me show you the way," said Cilan.

Ash, Pikachu, Iris, and Axew followed Cilan into a big building.

"This is the Gym?" Ash said. It looked more like a restaurant than a place to battle!

Two young men who looked like waiters came over to the little group.

"Hi, I'm Chili," said the first.

"I'm Cress," said the second. "Can we take your order?"

"Together, my brothers and I are the Gym Leaders of the Striaton City Gym," Cilan explained.

"Whoa, three Gym Leaders?!" said Ash.

"Select your opponent! You can battle any one of us!" Cilan said.

"Time to meet our Pokémon! Pansear, bring some heat!" Chili said, tossing his Poké Ball.

"*Pansear!*" Pansear cried.

"Pansear, the High Temp Pokémon," said Ash's Pokédex. "The tuft on its head can reach 600 degrees when it's angry."

"Pansage, here we go!" cried Cilan, tossing his Poké Ball.

"*Pansage!*" Pansage said.

"Pansage, the Grass Monkey Pokémon," said Ash's Pokédex. "The leaves on its head relieve stress."

"Panpour, make a splash!" Cress said, tossing his Poké Ball.

"*Panpour!*" Panpour cheered.

"Panpour, the Spray Pokémon," said Ash's Pokédex. "It can store water in the tufts on top of its head."

"I want to battle all of you!" Ash said.

Cilan was surprised. "Well, well, we've never met a Trainer quite like you!"

"Okay, Ash, but you have to win two out of three matches to earn our Gym badge," Cress decided.

First up: Chili and Pansear. Ash
surprised everyone by choosing Tepig.

"Tepig? Wouldn't a Water-type, like
Oshawott, be a better choice?" Iris
wondered.

"I promised Tepig it would be in my
first Unova Gym battle!" Ash explained.

Cilan announced the start of the match.

"Okay, Tepig, let's show them what you've got! Tackle, now!" Ash cheered.

"Tepig!" the little Pokémon yelled, running toward Pansear.

But Pansear dodged Tepig's Tackle.

Pansear blasted a Flamethrower attack back at Tepig. Then Pansear used Dig to knock Tepig off-balance. "Pansear's Dig is really strong! Tepig, run fast!" Ash hollered.

Pansear used Dig again. This time, Tepig was ready. It grabbed onto Pansear's tail and spun it around and around.

"Pansea-ah-er-ah-er!" Pansear was getting dizzy.

"All right, Tepig, use Tackle," Ash cheered.

"*Tepiiiiiiig!*" Tepig yelped as it made the winning move.

Cilan called the match. Ash had won!

But he still had two more brothers to battle.

Ash chose Pikachu to battle Cress and Panpour.

"Using an Electric-type against a Water-type. At least this match makes sense!" Iris said.

Pikachu started with Quick Attack. Panpour used Double Team and Scratch.

"All right, Pikachu! Thunderbolt, go!" Ash said.

"*Piiiika!*" Pikachu cried.

But Panpour whacked Pikachu with Scratch.

Pikachu countered with Volt Tackle.

"Now, Panpour, use Mud Sport!" Cress yelled.

"Panpooooour!" Panpour shouted. Pikachu slipped and fell in the mud.

"Finish this up with Water Gun!" Cress shouted.

That was it for Pikachu. Cress and Panpour had won the second match!

"You did your best!" Ash said.

If Ash wanted to earn his Gym
badge, he had to win the final battle
with Cilan.

"Oshawott, I choose you!" Ash said.

"A Flying-type would be better to
battle a Grass-type," Iris said.

"*Osha?*" Oshawott wondered if she
was right.

"Don't you remember rescuing Pikachu and Axew when they were in trouble?" Ash asked his little Water-type. "Show me that strength now!"

"*Oshawott!*" replied his Pokémon, ready to battle.

But before Oshawott could make a move, Pansage nailed it with Bullet Seed.

Oshawott kept missing Pansage with its Water Gun.

"Oshawoooott!" it sighed.

"Looks like you and Oshawott need to grow up a bit," Cilan said.

That made Ash a little angry! "Oshawott, Water Gun!" Ash cried. "You gotta aim better. You can do it!"

"Osha, osha, oshaaaa!" his Pokémon yelped. It finally got its aim right.

"Yes! That was a great attack!" Ash cheered.

"Time for some fun with the sun," said Cilan. "Pansage, use SolarBeam!"

Pansage launched a giant light beam at Oshawott.

Iris's jaw dropped. "Wow!"

"Quick, Oshawott, deflect it!"
Ash yelled.

Oshawott removed the scalchop
from its belly and held it up high.

Zap! Pansage's SolarBeam
bounced right off the scalchop.

"Oshawott, that was amazing!"
Ash cheered.

Pansage used Bullet Seed to knock the scalchop out of Oshawott's paw. It fell to the ground.

"Your battle style has no spice!" Cilan told Ash. "Keep on using Bullet Seed, Pansage."

Ash had an idea! He told Oshawott to hit the wall with Water Gun.

Oshawott's Water Gun bounced off the wall and hit the scalchop. It flew into the air. Oshawott caught it — and used it deflect Pansage's attack!

"Great job, Oshawott!" Ash yelled.

"Well, well, you do have some flavor after all!" Cilan said.

"Now use Razor Shell," Ash told his Pokémon.

Kapow! Just like that, Oshawott won the battle.

"Yeah! We did it, Oshawott!" Ash cheered.

"Pika, pika!" Pikachu agreed.

"This Badge is proof that you beat the Striaton City Gym," Chili said.

"It's called the Tri Badge," said Cilan.

"Thanks! My first badge in the Unova region!" Ash said proudly.

"Pika, pika!" Pikachu cheered.

Ash thanked the three brothers and left the Gym. Cilan chased after him.

"Wait, Ash! Can I join you on your journey?" Cilan asked.

"Yeah! Let's travel together," Ash said.

"Why don't we all go together?"
Cilan turned to Iris. "The three of us
are the recipe for a winning team!"

"Count me in!" Iris said.

"All right!" Ash cheered.

With friends old and new by his
side, Ash was excited for his next
adventure in Unova.